ABOUT THE AUTHOR

Phyllis Arkle was born and educated in Chester. As well as being the author of six Railway Cat titles she also wrote, *Magic at Midnight*, *Midnight in the Air*, *The Village Dinosaur* and *Two Village Dinosaurs*. Sadly, Phyllis Arkle died in 1997.

The Railway Cat
and the Horse

Phyllis Arkle

Illustrated by Stephanie Hawken

Hodder
Children's
Books

a division of Hodder Headline plc

Text copyright © 1987 Phyllis Arkle
Illustrations copyright © 1999 Stephanie Hawken

First published in 1987 by Hodder & Stoughton Children's Books

Published in paperback in 1988 by Puffin Books
This paperback edition published in 1999
by Hodder Children's Books

A Catalogue record for this book is available from the
British Library

ISBN 0 340 73214 8

Typeset by Avon Dataset Ltd, Bidford-on-Avon, Warks

Printed and bound in Great Britain by
The Guernsey Press Co. Ltd, Channel Isles

Hodder Children's Books
A Division of Hodder Headline plc
338 Euston Road
London NW1 3BH

Contents

1

An Important Consignment

Mustn't miss anything, thought Alfie the railway cat, as he ran towards a group of station staff assembled on platform No 2.

'Ah, good. All present now you're here, Alfie,' said Fred, the Chargeman, who was Alfie's special friend. 'Listening, everyone? I'm expecting an important consignment from the west country later today. Extra care will be required in unloading.'

'Aren't we busy enough as it is?' grumbled Leading Railman Hack. 'We should be paid extra for dealing with awkward jobs.'

Really! One never knew how that man was going to behave, thought Alfie. One minute complaining, next minute nice as pie.

'Tell us what it is, Fred,' said Brown, the Booking Clerk.

'Well . . . er . . . it's . . . er . . . it's . . .' mumbled Fred.

'Out with it,' said Hack impatiently.

'It's a horse,' said Fred smiling.

'A *horse!*' repeated Hack. 'But horses are not conveyed by rail nowadays.'

'Er . . . not usually,' said Fred, 'but this is rather special.'

'Probably a racehorse on its way to the Mead training stables,' said Brown. 'It might be valuable.'

'Do you think so?' said Hack excitedly.

'It's certainly worth a lot of money,' said Fred still smiling. (Alfie noticed that his eyes were twinkling.)

Hack rubbed his hands together. 'I've always been a good judge of horses,' he said. 'It will be interesting to take a close look at this one.'

An Important Consignment

'What's its name?' asked Brown.

'Rex,' said Fred, with a hand to his mouth.

There was a buzz of excitement about the station all morning. 'We're waiting for delivery of a very fine horse,' said Hack to one passenger after another.

But the railway cat was puzzled as, from time to time, he caught sight of the amused expression on Fred's face – a sure sign that his friend had something up his sleeve!

Shortly after midday the staff, including Alfie, assembled on the Up platform.

'Here she comes!' shouted Hack as the train approached.

Waving his tail, Alfie rushed up and down the platform. The guard poked his head out and shouted, 'Hello, Alfie!'

'Miaow!' sang Alfie.

Hack moved forward.

'Hold on a minute, Hack,' said Fred. 'We are about to handle a very superior horse. Great care must be taken.'

'Hope he doesn't bite,' said Brown.

Fred laughed as he shook his head. Hack's eyes

scanned the length of the train as it drew up at the platform. 'There's no horse vehicle on this train,' he cried as he glanced accusingly at Fred.

'Er, no . . .' said Fred. He walked forward as the door of the guard's van was opened from inside. 'He's in here.'

'In the *guard's* van?' shouted Hack. 'Have you gone clean off your head?'

Alfie followed Fred into the van. 'Miaow!' he greeted the guard.

'Hello, Alfie,' said the guard. 'Come to meet Rex?'

'Miaow!' cried Alfie.

'Where is he?' demanded Hack as he leapt into the van. He took a quick look round and turned to Fred. 'Where is this wonder horse?' he sneered, his face red with annoyance. 'I believe you've been pulling my leg. There's no horse.'

'Oh, yes, there is,' said Fred. 'Calm down. We've got a job to do.'

Alfie followed Fred to a large wooden crate in a corner of the van. 'He's in here,' said Fred.

There was silence for a moment and Hack's eyes widened in disbelief. Alfie peered through a chink in the crate and, sure enough, saw part of a hoof and a foreleg. *But* – they were not flesh and blood limbs!

Alfie looked up at Fred. 'Miaow!' he cried. It's very naughty of you to tease Hack.

'Come off it, Fred,' cried Hack. 'Admit it, there's no horse.'

'But there is,' insisted Fred. 'I never said it was a racehorse. It's an old rocking-horse, which aroused interest when it appeared in a television series recently.'

For once Hack was dumbfounded, while Alfie rolled over and over at Fred's feet. Of course, he should have guessed! Only this morning he had overheard Fred talking on the telephone to old Mr Brock, the rocking-horse mender.

'Come on, everyone, lend a hand,' ordered Fred. 'The van's waiting outside to take Rex to Mr Brock's. By rights we should have a security guard with us.'

'You're kidding!' cried Hack.

'No, seriously,' said Fred. 'No one knows Rex's age, but he has been owned by several genera-tions of the same family and there's a lot of interest in old rocking-horses at present.'

'No interest to me,' said Hack sourly. Reluctantly he moved forward to help unload.

Alfie decided he would be first at Mr Brock's to welcome Rex. Off he ran and covered the half mile to the workshop in record time. As he trotted down the passage at the side of the house, where Mr Brock lived alone, he breathed in a lovely familiar mixed-up smell of leather soap, polish, oil and paint coming from the workshop at the end of the passage.

Alfie halted in the open doorway. Brush in hand, the rocking-horse mender stood in the middle of the workshop putting a coat of paint on a large rocking-horse. Around him were rocking-horses of all sizes, some on rockers, others on swingers.

Some of the horses were waiting to be repainted, some had saddle or harness missing, while others were short of an eye, an ear, a tail or a mane. Many of them were like old friends to Alfie as they had been in the workshop for a long time. The railway cat was a regular visitor at Mr Brock's.

The old man looked up. 'Hello, Alfie!' he cried. 'I'm glad to see you. Taking a rest from station duties?'

'Miaow!' said Alfie as, purring loudly, he leapt forward and rubbed against Mr Brock's legs.

There was the sound of a vehicle braking

outside. Hurriedly Mr Brock put down his brush. 'Ah, good!' he exclaimed as he made for the door. 'That must be Rex. This is going to be the most interesting restoration job I have ever undertaken.'

Very excited, Alfie followed him back down the passage and into the road, where Fred and Hack were helping the van driver manoeuvre the crate out of the van and on to a trolley.

Mr Brock dithered about, got in the way and issued advice, until Fred patted his shoulder and said kindly, 'Leave it to us, Mr Brock.'

The passage was just wide enough to take the trolley. 'There's really no need for three of us to move this thing,' protested Hack. He stumbled across Alfie and scraped the crate against the wall.

'It's that cat's fault,' he yelled. 'Makes my blood boil the way he belts about like a rocket.'

'Oh, dear! Oh, dear!' moaned Mr Brock. 'Do be careful, please, Hack. Rex must come to no harm. In my opinion he could be very valuable and I'm nervous of having him in my charge.'

The rocking-horse mender ran ahead into the

workshop and moved some of the horses to make a space for Rex. The crate was wheeled inside. It was soon opened and the rocking-horse was revealed. Everyone stared, for Rex was a sorry sight. Two hundred years' wear and tear showed only too plainly. The horse's legs, which were stretched at full gallop, were damaged. There was a faded red saddle on his back and the tattered remains of a leather bridle hung from his jaws.

A few strands of gingery hair were all that remained of the mane and tail. The body was a dull grey with brown splotches here and there, relieved only by a white diamond on the forehead. No matter, thought Alfie. He knew that with great skill and patience Mr Brock would turn Rex into a beautiful creature again.

But, 'Huh! Call that thing valuable?' jeered Hack. 'I've seen better articles in a junk shop.'

'Brrr . . . rr . . . rr . . .' growled Alfie. Rude man, Hack.

'You'll have to eat your words when Mr Brock has finished working on Rex,' said Fred.

The rocking-horse mender smiled and nodded as he gently stroked the horse and moved him to and fro on the long rockers. 'Many children have enjoyed riding Rex,' he murmured. 'Now, sadly, Mr Stanley, his present owner, is forced to sell him, along with other family heirlooms.'

'But why?' asked Fred.

'To raise enough money to repair the family's old mansion, otherwise that too will have to be sold,' sighed Mr Brock.

'What a pity,' said Fred. 'Cheer up, Mr Brock. Hack and I will have to go back to work, but I'll leave Alfie with you, if you wish.'

'Oh, thank you, Fred,' said the old man. 'I'm always pleased to have Alfie's company when you can spare him.'

'We can *always* spare . . .' began Hack.

'Now then, Hack,' Fred interrupted. 'Just give a hand with the crate.'

They both moved the crate into a corner before leaving Mr Brock's workshop.

'Prrr . . . rr . . . rr . . . rr . . .' sang Alfie happily. It was lunch time and he was always sure of a tit-bit or two from his old friend, the rocking-horse mender, who was particularly good with a lean bacon and cheese fry.

2

Alfie is Worried

On his return to the station Alfie found an ill-tempered Hack in charge. As he didn't want the station to get a bad name the railway cat made himself very pleasant to passengers. During the afternoon a smartly dressed man stepped from a London train. He bent down and tickled Alfie under the chin.

'Miaow!' said Alfie as he flopped on to his back and rolled his head, inviting more attention.

Hack came along. 'Always sucking up to

people, that cat,' he said scornfully.

The man glanced up. 'Please direct me to the rocking-horse mender's workshop,' he said.

'And what do *you* want with Mr Brock?' asked Hack suspiciously.

'That's none of your business,' was the firm reply.

'Oh, yes it is!' retorted Hack. 'There's a valuable hor . . .' He stopped short. 'Anyhow, *I'm* boss here until Fred comes back, and I'm telling you nothing.'

'And *I'm* a senior Government official on private business,' said the man glaring at Hack.

'Ho! Ho! Expect me to believe that,' shouted Hack. 'I've heard of your sort. You're up to no good, I'm sure of that.'

At that moment Fred came running down the stairs. 'Sir!' he gasped. 'I'm sorry, but I've only just received a message about your visit.'

Hack went red in the face and put a hand to his mouth. Fred glanced from one to the other. 'Is anything wrong?' he asked.

'There is,' said the Government official. 'I asked this man a civil question and received a very rude response. He must be reported for insolence. But in the meantime please tell me the way to the rocking-horse mender's workshop.'

'Certainly, sir,' said Fred as he led the way to the front of the station.

'I was only trying to protect the old horse,' said Hack furiously to no one in particular.

'Miaow!' said Alfie quietly. I know you were.

When Fred came back he was very annoyed and gave Hack a good ticking off. 'Just show better judgement in future,' he advised, 'and don't dare be rude to *any* passenger.'

Hack stuck his hands in his pockets and kicked at a platform seat.

'Stop that!' shouted Fred.

'I was only thinking of Rex,' said Hack. 'That man might not be genuine.'

'Nonsense!' said Fred. 'He's what he said he is, a senior Government official. Stop playing at being a detective and get on with your real duties.'

Hack went about all day looking very aggrieved. Alfie felt sorry for him. Anyone could make a mistake, couldn't they? When later in the day the official returned to the station to catch a London train, Alfie made him very welcome. Hack hovered about nearby and when the train arrived at the platform he rushed forward and opened a door for the man. 'I'm sorry I was uncivil, sir,' he said.

'That's all right, forget it this time,' said the man. 'But watch your step in future.'

That night Alfie, unable to sleep, moved restlessly in his basket. He was worried. If Rex was really valuable would someone try to steal him in the middle of the night while Mr Brock slept in his house?

Eventually Alfie gave up trying to settle down. He left the waiting room by climbing through a ventilator in the window and made his way to Mr Brock's. He crept down the passage at the side of the house, stopping now and then to listen. The only sound was an owl hooting in a nearby copse. Silently Alfie leapt on to a window sill and gazed into the workshop.

Having very good eyesight and helped by light from the moon, he could just make out Rex's shadowy form surrounded by the other rocking-horses. Alfie stayed for a while, listening and looking. It was very quiet. Satisfied that all was well, he was about to jump down when, from inside the workshop, he heard a sort of grunting noise. He peered through the window and saw something moving on the floor near Rex.

Alfie's fears were justified – BURGLARS, he thought! Flustered, he looked round for a possible entrance into the workshop and noticed a small ventilator in the window. He was used to ventilators so, with no great effort, he stretched up and slipped into the workshop.

Ears back and tail quivering, he moved very very slowly across the floor towards Rex. With tensed muscles, he crouched down before springing at a figure on the floor alongside the old horse.

There was a yell and a scream as Alfie landed right on top of someone lying on a camp bed. The bed collapsed and Alfie found himself on the floor by a man.

'Oh! Oh! Oh!' shrieked the man, and what a surprise Alfie had, for the voice was *Mr Brock's!* The old man lashed out and hit Alfie on the nose.

'Mia . . . ow . . . ow . . .' moaned Alfie as he lay sprawled on the floor. It's only me!

'Oh, dear, is that you, Alfie?' gasped Mr Brock as he put out a hand to calm the railway cat. 'You did give me a terrible fright. My heart's beating like a hammer. I'll have to lie quiet for a while.'

Alfie stretched out beside his friend and purred encouragingly. It took at least half an hour for Mr Brock to recover from the shock. At last he managed to laugh. 'Really, Alfie!' he

Alfie is Worried

cried. 'Here am I doing my best to guard Rex night and day, and I am attacked by one of my very good friends.'

'Miaow!' said Alfie. I'm sorry.

'Never mind,' said Mr Brock. He shook off the rumpled blankets covering him and got to his feet. 'I'm sure you didn't mean to frighten me.' He switched on the light and looked down at the camp bed, flat on the floor. 'I'll have to get this bed to rights first.'

Alfie watched as the old man struggled to

put the bed and blankets into position again. When this had been done Mr Brock stood back panting. 'Now, Alfie,' he said, 'shall we have a drink together before we try to get some sleep?'

Mr Brock picked up a thermos flask from a table and poured some milky coffee into a saucer, which he put on the floor. 'There you are, Alfie,' he said.

Alfie waited politely. 'Now one for me,' said Mr Brock as he filled a cup from the flask. 'Cheers, Alfie!' he said as he raised the cup.

'Miaow!' said Alfie. He put down his head and lapped noisily. He was very fond of milky coffee.

Mr Brock switched off the light and got back into bed. 'Come on, Alfie,' he said. 'There's room for you.'

Alfie wasted no time in accepting the invitation by leaping on to the bed. 'Careful!' cried Mr Brock in alarm. 'You'll have us both on the floor again.'

Alfie kneaded the top blanket with his paws and followed his tail in a circle several times before he settled down with a flop in the curve of Mr Brock's legs.

'I'll be unable to move for the rest of the night,' laughed Mr Brock, 'but you'll keep me nice and warm, Alfie.'

They were quiet for a time, then Mr Brock started to talk to himself, and to Alfie. 'Had a Government man in this morning. He wanted to know all about Rex, where he came from, when he was going to be sold, etc. The man is eager to buy Rex for his private antique collection but, regretfully, I had to tell him I'm certain he would be out-bid at auction.'

The old man sighed as he pulled the bedclothes over his shoulders and nearly dislodged Alfie. 'Such a pity,' he said. 'I'm so afraid a foreigner will make the highest bid and Rex will be taken out of this country.'

Mr Brock's eyes closed and he started to wheeze and then to snore softly. Before Alfie drifted off to sleep he gazed round at the horses. They looked so alert, almost alive, in the moonlight that Alfie imagined they might all gallop off along a moonbeam. Silly, he told himself! The railway cat's eyes closed and he dreamed he was rocking, rocking, rocking.

Mr Brock was an early riser. 'I'll just go along to the house for a wash and brush-up and breakfast, before I start work on Rex,' he said. 'I've put a little minced beef aside for you, so come along, Alfie.'

Back in the workshop after breakfast Alfie watched Mr Brock at work on Rex. First the faded red saddle and leather bridle were removed, then the straggly mane and tail were cut off.

'I'll have to strip off all the old paint first,' said the rocking-horse mender. 'The ears need mending and the legs strengthening. Believe me, there's a great deal of work to be done before Rex is restored to my satisfaction.'

After a while Mr Brock looked at his watch. 'How time flies,' he said. 'Fred will be watching out for you. You'd better be off, Alfie.'

Mr Brock opened the door. Alfie took the hint and, with a flick of his tail, disappeared down the passage.

'Our Alfie's turned up like a bad penny,' cried Hack when Alfie arrived at the station.

Alfie is Worried

'Like a very good penny,' Fred corrected, as he bent down and tickled the railway cat. 'Passengers have been enquiring about you, Alfie. Ready for breakfast?'

'Miaow!' said Alfie. Thank you. Two breakfasts are always better than one!

The station was very busy. So many trains to meet, just as many to see away and parcels to be handled. To and fro over the bridge went Alfie all day. Fred was shutting the main gate after the last train had departed, when a very tired cat ran past him.

'Hey, Alfie, come back!' yelled Fred. 'Where are you off to now?'

'Miaow!' cried Alfie over his shoulder. I'm going to keep guard with Mr Brock of course.

The rocking-horse mender was just about to lock up for the night when Alfie appeared. 'Thought you'd come along,' said Mr Brock. 'I'm very glad to see you, but I do hope we sleep soundly tonight.

Once in bed it didn't take them long to fall fast asleep as the horses kept watch round them, and nothing disturbed them that night.

3

Hack is Worried

After a good night's sleep Alfie felt ready for
anything. He left Mr Brock's early and ran back
to the station to be first on duty.

Hack came next and unlocked the staff room
door. 'Hungry, eh, Alfie?' he asked as he went
to the cupboard. 'Won't keep you waiting
long.'

Alfie blinked in surprise. Hack had evidently
heeded Fred's stern words about his behaviour.
The Leading Railman was polite to everyone all
morning. In fact, it was a pleasure to work

alongside him, thought Alfie, as he bustled about among the passengers.

About midday two men, last to leave a train from London, stopped to speak to Hack at the gate. They asked many questions about passengers and traffic. Hack was very civil but was reluctant to answer so many queries. He looked round for Fred, who was not in sight.

'Miaow?' said Alfie as he stared hard at the men. Why do you want to know so much about our railway?

At last one of the men glanced cautiously over his shoulder before speaking. 'Confidentially,' he began in a whisper, 'we are part of the railway fraud squad . . .'

'Miaow!' interrupted Alfie, alarmed. No need to take *my* paw marks, I've done nothing wrong.

'. . . looking out for fare dodgers and other criminals.'

'Oh well, that's different,' said Hack relieved.

'For instance,' the man continued, 'have you handled any freight lately that might attract attention?'

'No, I don't think so,' said Hack, 'just the

usual mail bags and parcels.' He thought for a moment. 'There's Rex, of course, the valuable old rocking-horse Mr Brock is mending.'

'Really? How interesting. We won't miss the opportunity of visiting Mr Brock. Where does he live?' said the other man.

'Miaow!' cried Alfie, who had taken an instinctive dislike to both men. Don't tell them, Hack!

But to Alfie's dismay Hack gave the men precise directions to the rocking-horse mender's workshop.

'Thank you,' said the first man. 'We won't forget to mention your name at headquarters for being courteous and helpful. You might even get promotion.'

Hack looked very pleased with himself. The men set off and after them went Alfie. Arriving opposite Mr Brock's, the men stared at the house as they strolled past. From a nearby doorway Alfie watched as they turned and walked back, stopping to take a longer look at the house and peering down the passage. Then they nodded to one another as if in satisfaction and returned to the village.

Now why hadn't they visited Mr Brock as they had said they would, thought Alfie? He felt very uneasy all afternoon and he kept out of the way when Hack saw the men off on the early evening London train. Alfie hoped he'd never see either of them again.

Determined not to leave Mr Brock on his own for one single night while Rex was with him, Alfie went along to the workshop after the last train had left the station. 'I don't know what I'd do without you,' said Mr Brock as he opened the door for Alfie. 'But don't keep scratching the door. Just miaow. I'll hear you.'

It wasn't long before they were both in bed. Mr Brock fell asleep almost as soon as his head touched the pillow, but Alfie was fidgety, and moonlight streaming in through the window kept him awake. He jerked his head at every slight sound and he wriggled about constantly.

At last the old man opened his eyes and said, 'Oh, *please*, Alfie, lie still or neither of us will have a wink of sleep all night.'

Alfie didn't move for a while but he stayed on the alert. Then, just as he was dozing off, he heard a faint noise outside. Someone moving about? Cautiously he raised his head and saw a shadow pass the window. He waited, trembling. Whoever it was returned and stared into the workshop.

'Miaow!' said Alfie quietly, as he crawled up the bed and pawed Mr Brock's shoulder. The old man refused to move, so Alfie pulled at his pyjama jacket until he opened one eye.

'Oh, dear, what's the matter now, Alfie?' he sighed. He raised himself on one elbow and as he was facing the window, immediately caught sight of the figure outside.

Resourcefully, he picked up a thick stick which was lying on the floor beside the bed. 'I'm ready for anyone who dares enter my workshop,' he whispered as, followed by Alfie, he crept across the floor towards the door. The figure at the window had disappeared. Mr Brock clutched the stick as he and Alfie stood behind the door and listened. There was silence.

'Probably just some petty thief slinking about said Mr Brock after a time. 'I'll report the matter to the police tomorrow. We might as well lie down again.'

He turned towards the bed, but suddenly there were sounds of a struggle outside and they heard a shout, 'Got you!'

'That's Constable Pringle's voice!' cried Mr

Brock. 'He promised to keep a special watch on my premises.'

The scuffle outside continued. 'I must go to his aid,' shouted Mr Brock. He unlocked the door and darted out brandishing the stick. Alfie peered round the doorway and saw two forms, one in uniform, locked in a struggle.

Mr Brock joined in the fray. He lifted the stick high towards the intruder and, missing his aim, caught the policeman a glancing blow on the side of his head.

'Miaow!' howled Alfie as Constable Pringle

went down like a ninepin. Now you've done it, Mr Brock. Striking a policeman – a *real* crime! And you've knocked off his hat as well.

To Alfie's relief, the constable, holding his head got swiftly to his feet and cried out, 'Catch him, Mr Brock – don't let him get away!'

The rocking-horse mender swung round and grabbed the man who, strangely, had not attempted to run off. 'I'm holding him,' shouted Mr Brock. Alfie ran out of the workshop and joined the group. For the first time they all got a good view of the man in Mr Brock's grasp.

'Why! Would you believe it? It's *Hack*!' gasped the rocking-horse mender.

'Miaow!' said Alfie. So it is!

'May I ask what you are doing here?' asked Constable Pringle severely.

Hack looked very embarrassed. 'Well, er . . . thinking about it afterwards, I was worried about the intentions of two men who asked a lot of questions at the station this morning,' he said trembling. 'So I came along just in case Mr Brock needed help.'

'It's not your job to keep watch on Mr Brock,

said the constable, 'and in any case you are trespassing on private property.'

'I'm sure Hack had my interests at heart,' said Mr Brock. He looked nervously at the bump which had appeared on the constable's head. 'And, my goodness, I didn't intend hitting *you*, Constable. It was all a mistake.'

'Never mind about that now,' said the constable. 'It's all in the course of duty.' He picked up his hat.

'Shall we go inside?' suggested the rocking-horse mender.

In the workshop the three men talked things over, while Alfie listened. Constable Pringle said it was his duty to report the matter, but he was sure that, in the circumstances, a lenient view would be taken of Mr Brock striking a policeman and of Hack prowling round in the middle of the night.

'But don't do such a stupid thing again, Hack,' warned the constable. '*We'll* look after Mr Brock, there's no need for you to interfere.'

'I'm very lucky,' said Mr Brock. 'Police keeping guard outside, and Alfie inside for company.'

Eventually the constable and Hack departed and Mr Brock and Alfie went back to bed, only to toss and turn for what was left of the night.

Next morning back at the station Alfie found Hack going about his duties with a worried, resentful expression on his face. Not for the first time Alfie felt sorry for him. He was sure that Hack had only acted out of concern for the rocking-horse mender.

Later on Alfie was relieved when he overheard Fred telling Hack that the police had decided to overlook the little matter of trespassing by Hack, and the more serious one of Mr Brock hitting a policeman.

'But, for goodness sake, Hack, pull yourself together and let's have no more nonsense of this sort,' said Fred. 'I'll be in the office if you want me.' Off he went.

It was quiet at the station and Hack sat down on a platform seat. Alfie jumped up on to the seat and sat down beside him. The railway cat was surprised when Hack started to talk to him. 'Fact is, Alfie,' he said. 'I never know when I'm doing the right thing.'

'Miaow!' said Alfie. I know *exactly* how you feel!

Hack absently stroked Alfie. Then he put a hand into a pocket and pulled out a ping-pong ball. Alfie looked up at Hack, then down at the ball. Could it be possible? Was Hack really going to play games?

'Found this in a compartment,' said Hack. 'Catch, Alfie!' He threw the ball right to the top of the bridge steps. Alfie sprang up as if released from a catapult, and was up the steps in no time at all. He followed the ball as it bounced down, step by step, on to the platform where he had a strenuous time trying to catch it. When he did manage to touch the ball he found he couldn't hold on to it and off it went, bouncing along the platform.

'Miaow!' said Alfie looking up at Hack, who was laughing at the railway cat's antics.

Hack bent down and picked up the ball. He was about to throw it up the steps again when the first passenger for the next train arrived. Hack hastily put it into his pocket. 'Another time, Alfie,' he whispered.

The Railway Cat and the Horse

'Miaow!' said Alfie. I'm very glad to know you can play games.

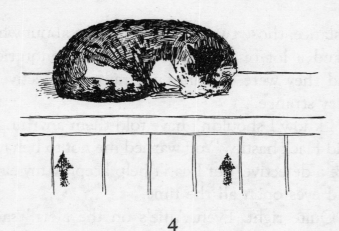

4

Ghost-ridden!

Alfie continued to spend nights with Mr Brock and he often popped into the workshop during the day.

'Like a cat on hot bricks, our Alfie,' said Hack. 'Here one minute, off to Mr Brock's the next.'

'Alfie is rather restless,' admitted Fred. 'He probably senses our concern about Rex's safety. Cats are remarkable creatures.'

'You can say that again!' cried Hack.

'It seems to me rocking-horses are very much in the news at present,' Fred went on. 'For instance, those two men you told me about who asked a lot of questions. I've made enquiries and they were certainly not railway detectives. Very strange.'

'I know I shouldn't have told them anything,' said Hack hastily. 'You warned me not to behave like a detective, but I can't help keeping my ears and eyes open all the time.'

'Quite right. Even Alfie's on the alert!' said Fred.

'Miaow!' agreed Alfie.

Alfie watched Hack as the Leading Railman closely studied every stranger who appeared at the station, and even stared hard at the regular passengers.

One man grumbled to Fred, 'Why is Hack acting as if he suspects one of us might have the crown jewels stuffed under our jacket?'

Fred laughed. 'Oh, take no notice,' he said. 'We've all got something on our minds at present.'

One day on arriving at the workshop Alfie found Mr Brock very upset. 'Alfie,' said the old man. 'I'm convinced someone has been in my workshop without permission. Earlier this morning I locked the door and secured the window before going out for a short while. When I came back I found my brushes and tools had been tampered with.'

'Miaow!' said Alfie alarmed.

He glanced up at the window. 'Miaow!' he said again. No one, except me, could squeeze through that ventilator.

'How did someone get in? And out again?' said Mr Brock. 'It's ghostly! But, thank goodness, Rex hasn't been harmed.' He sighed. 'How I shall miss that horse, but how relieved I shall be to see him safely on his way. Ah well, back to work.'

The old man reached up and took down a tin of primer from a shelf. 'There's very little more work to be done on Rex,' he said. 'I hope to give him the final touches before the week is out.'

'Miaow!' said Alfie. That means only a few more days of anxiety.

Just then there was a knock on the door. They both jumped. In walked the postman.

'Whatever's the matter?' he asked as he caught sight of the startled look on Mr Brock's face.

'I'm almost distracted,' said Mr Brock, and he told the postman what had happened, adding, 'but no damage has been done and, so far as I can tell, nothing has been stolen.' He shook his head. 'It's a mystery.'

'Well, if it's Rex you're worried about,' said the postman, 'it's my opinion that it would be very difficult for anyone to steal him and eventually sell him without being traced.'

'That's true,' sighed Mr Brock. 'But there are

some very clever, dishonest people about nowadays. When I was a lad . . .'

'Yes, yes, Mr Brock,' interrupted the postman hastily. 'I know. It was different then. Sorry I can't stay for a chat, but I've a very large round today. See you tomorrow.' He waved to Alfie as he went out.

Mr Brock worked hard for the rest of the day and Alfie stayed with him most of the time. Sleep didn't come easily that night as they lay on the camp bed. Had someone really managed to break into the workshop while Mr Brock was out? If so, what could he, or she, be interested in, if not Rex?

Alfie was relieved when the first grey light of dawn shone through the window. He was back early at the station. He found passengers and staff content because trains were running to time and everything looked neat and tidy. For once, the platforms had been properly swept by Hack.

Fred came on duty. 'Hello, Alfie,' he said. 'How is Mr Brock getting on with Rex?'

'Hope he won't take much longer,' Hack put in, 'or we'll all be nervous wrecks.'

'Not as bad as that, surely?' laughed Fred. He held out a parcel. 'Hack, will you please take this along to the workshop. Mr Brock's waiting for it.'

Hack set off with the parcel and Alfie followed. Mr Brock greeted them at the workshop door. He was more disturbed than Alfie had ever seen him. 'Someone has been in *again*!' he cried.

'Have you informed the police?' asked Hack.

'I mentioned the matter to Constable Pringle when he called yesterday,' was the answer.

'Well, I should get in touch with him again, immediately,' said Hack.

'I'll take your advice,' said the rocking-horse mender. 'Will you please stay on guard with Alfie while I go and phone from the house.' He was already halfway down the passage.

'Don't worry, Rex will be in safe hands so long as I'm about,' Hack called after him. Hands in pockets he stood just outside the door and kept turning his head from side to side as he kept a sharp look-out.

Alfie suddenly pricked up his ears as he heard

a slight sound from inside the workshop. He glanced quickly at Hack, who had obviously heard nothing. Quickly Alfie streaked into the workshop. He stopped short for, standing by Rex, were two dirty-looking children, a boy and a girl.

The children giggled and hunched their shoulders when they saw Alfie. 'Sssh!' said the boy with finger to lip.

Alfie's tail flicked as Mr Brock's footsteps were heard approaching. With a whispered, 'Let's have a bit of fun, shall we?' the boy started to push Rex vigorously. The girl joined in. Backwards and forwards went the horse, rearing higher and higher until he appeared to Alfie to be in danger of rocking right over.

Then the children rushed across the workshop and squeezed behind the crate standing in a corner. Just as Hack was about to step inside, Alfie ran after the children and pushed in between their legs. He poked his head round the side of the crate.

Hack strolled in, stopped in his tracks, gasped and put a hand to his mouth. His eyes widened in fright as he stared at Rex still rocking violently.

'Ahh . . . ahh . . . ahh . . . ' he yelled as he turned back and nearly knocked Mr Brock over.

'Hey, look where you're going, Hack!' protested the old man. 'What's the trouble?'

Hack gulped. 'This pl . . . pl . . . place must be haun . . . haun . . . haunted,' he stammered. 'Look!'

Apprehensively Mr Brock peered into the workshop. 'Rex is rocking . . .' he began in amazement.

'. . . On his own!' Hack pointed out. '*He's being ridden by a ghost!* Let's scram.'

But Mr Brock grasped his arm. 'Non . . . nonsense, Hack,' he said, in a trembling voice. 'There must be a rational explanation.' They watched for a few seconds, then Mr Brock cried, 'He's slowing down.'

'Th . . . th . . . that's because we're looking at him,' said Hack.

At that moment Mr Brock caught sight of two round bright eyes staring at him. 'There's Alfie behind the crate!' he exclaimed.

Ghost-ridden!

'Oh! Might have guessed that cat would have a paw in this,' cried Hack exasperated. 'Wouldn't surprise me if any minute he swished past us on a broomstick.'

Still holding on to Hack, Mr Brock led the way towards the corner. As they crept nearer they heard a muffled sound. Both men dashed forward and pulled the crate away from the wall. And there crouched the children. Before they could escape Mr Brock grabbed the boy, and Hack the girl.

'Who are you?' asked Mr Brock as he shook the boy slightly.

'I'm Robin,' was the reply, 'and she's my sister, Sara. We're twins and we've come to live at the bottom of your garden.'

'Really?' said Mr Brock. He turned to Hack. 'I've been so busy working on Rex I haven't had time even to enquire about my new neighbours.'

'But how did you manage to get in?' Hack wanted to know.

'Easy,' said Robin. He pointed at the old-fashioned disused fireplace. 'Down there. It's wide and there are plenty of bricks sticking out to use as handholds and footholds.'

'Well I never!' cried an astonished Mr Brock as he gazed at the twins. 'And it's very dirty in there.'

Sara broke in eagerly. 'We wanted so much to see Rex as we had heard people talking about him, but we were ordered not to bother you.'

Mr Brock smiled. 'Well, I can understand you wanting to have a look at the old horse, but you

must ask my permission *first*.' He pushed the children forward. 'Here are your ghosts, Hack.'

'Oh, they didn't fool *me*,' said Hack loudly. 'I was only joking about the workshop being haunted.'

Mr Brock smiled again and Alfie cried, 'Miaow!' Oh, no, you weren't joking!

'Would you like a ride on Rex?' Mr Brock asked the children.

'Please!' they cried in unison.

'And Alfie?' said Sara.

Robin and Sara climbed on to Rex's back. 'Now Alfie,' said Mr Brock as he lifted the railway cat and placed him in front of the twins. 'Rex is strong enough to carry you all,' he said proudly.

The door opened and in came Constable Pringle. 'Ho–ho!' he cried, surprised. 'What's going on? I thought you were in trouble, Mr Brock.'

'Oh, I'm sorry to have bothered you, Constable,' said Mr Brock as he continued to push Rex. 'It was a false alarm.'

'Well, we're certainly getting used to those,'

said the constable.

After the ride the children were sent off home – through the workshop door!

That night before going to sleep Alfie glanced at Rex bathed in moonlight, with the other rocking-horses all round him. Just then Alfie couldn't really blame Hack for believing in ghosts . . .

5

A False Alarm

Twice the next day Alfie caught sight of the twins peeping round the door watching Mr Brock at work.

'Miaow!' cried Alfie loudly on the second occasion. Go away. Stop disturbing Mr Brock.

The old man looked up and the children scampered away. He shook his head. 'Very mischievous children,' he said. 'I'll have to keep everything under lock and key, in case they get in here again unobserved.'

'Miaow!' said Alfie. I'll keep an eye on them

for you. He followed the children home and squatted down outside the cottage. The twins' mother noticed him.

'That's a very fine-looking cat,' said Mrs Tucker.

'He's the station cat,' Robin told her.

'He's a magnificent cat,' added Sara.

Alfie stretched out, bent his head and rolled right over. Mrs Tucker invited him inside and gave him a slice of chicken. Alfie enjoyed all the fuss, but he didn't trust the children out of his sight for the rest of the day.

His vigil didn't cease when darkness fell. He wouldn't put it past the rascals sneaking out of the house when their parents were asleep. After a quick dash back to the station for supper, he returned to his post.

When the last light went out in the cottage the railway cat made his way via a shed roof to the window sill outside the twins' bedroom. The curtains were drawn and the window partly open.

To pass the time profitably Alfie kept a sharp lookout for anything moving. Once he crouched right down when he thought he saw a fox slinking across the garden, but it turned out to be a farm dog. Alfie stayed quite still for at least an hour, but the dog didn't return. Suddenly he became aware of movements inside the bedroom. He got to his feet when light from a torch flickered through the curtains.

The twins must be getting out of bed!

Putting his left ear close to the window pane Alfie heard whispering. 'Now's our best chance while they're asleep,' said Robin. 'We'll get the scissors and cut it up straight away before they can stop us.'

Alfie did not catch all of the rest of the conversation, but he did hear Sara mention Rex, and then giggle.

Alfie flattened his ears and growled in his throat. Cut it up? he thought. What? Surely they didn't intend damaging the old horse. Unthinkable! Yet there was something afoot and Rex might be harmed unintentionally.

Desperately Alfie started jumping against the window. He heard Sara gasp, but Robin said, 'It's all right, silly. I guess it's only Alfie.'

He drew back the curtains and stuck his head out of the window. 'Sshh, Alfie!' he whispered. 'We've got a job on hand, so be a good cat and leave us alone.'

Gently he pushed until Alfie was forced to jump down. How undignified! Alfie was furious at such treatment. He sat down outside the front door and waited uneasily for the twins to emerge with the scissors.

But nothing happened.

Mystified, he waited until sunrise before he ran back to the workshop, to be let in by Mr

Brock. 'I've missed you, Alfie,' said the old man. 'Have you been out all night?'

'Miaow!' said Alfie. I've been on guard duty. He accepted a cod's head and some milk before deciding to pay a brief visit to the station.

A second breakfast provided by Hack did nothing to calm his fears. Cut it up? Cut it up? kept going through his mind. Without staying even to wash himself he started off again, but Hack caught hold of his tail.

'Think Mr Brock can't manage without you, you conceited cat?' said the Leading Railman scornfully. 'Well, let me remind you, your job is to keep the vermin down on this station.' He grabbed Alfie and shut him in the staff room.

Alfie howled and howled until Fred came on duty and released him. Fred started to advise him, 'Now then, Alfie, Hack's got a point, you *are* the station cat and . . .'

But before Fred could move, the railway cat streaked between the man's legs and was off like a shot. Mr Brock was surprised to see him back so soon.

'I'll be unpopular with the station staff for

keeping you away from your station duties!' he exclaimed.

'Miaow!' cried Alfie. You might need the help of an intelligent cat like me soon!

There was no sign of the children during the morning. After lunch Alfie sat down and watched Mr Brock at work. He tried hard to keep alert, but his eyes closed, his head sank on to his chest and he fell asleep.

But he woke immediately when he heard someone outside the workshop. Robin's head appeared round the door.

Alfie sprang up and cried, 'MIAOW!'

Mr Brock looked up startled. 'What's the matter, Alfie?' he said. 'If those twins are lurking round here again, I'll have to think what to do with them!'

He waited for a while and then resumed work. After a time he put down his tool and told Alfie, 'Just going round to the back for cleansing fluid. You'll be in charge for exactly one minute.'

As soon as the rocking-horse mender's back was turned, Alfie was alarmed, but not surprised, when the twins rushed into the workshop. They each carried a bundle under one arm. They ran up to Rex. Robin quickly draped what appeared to be a tatty woollen cloth on top of the horse's head, while Sara pressed something similar on to his rump.

Mr Brock entered and stopped in amazement as he gazed at the horse.

'We thought Rex ought to have a new mane and tail,' Robin said eagerly, 'so we've made them specially for him.'

'I do hope you are pleased, Mr Brock,' said Sara anxiously.

Speechless, Mr Brock walked all round Rex, while the children stood by, beaming. 'Well . . .' he began at last, as he stroked his chin. 'It was . . . er . . . a very kind thought, but –'

Alfie jerked his head round as he heard someone enter the workshop. Mrs Tucker came forward. She stared at Rex. Her eyes glinted and her face was flushed. Alfie could tell that she was very annoyed. She might explode! The children backed away as she pointed at Rex.

'That's my *rug*!' she cried. (So *that's* what it is, thought Alfie.)

'But it's only an old rug,' wailed Sara, beginning to cry.

'Indeed it is,' said Mrs Tucker. 'It belonged to your great-grandmother.'

'I'm sure the children meant well,' said Mr Brock hastily. He turned to Robin. 'Have you kept the rest of the rug pieces?' he asked.

Robin nodded.

'Well then,' said the rocking-horse mender, 'I've got some very strong needles and, as soon as I've finished work on Rex, you two can help me sew the pieces together again. The old rug will look as good as new.'

The corners of Mrs Tucker's mouth started to twitch. 'That's very kind of you, Mr Brock,' she said. 'I'll agree, on condition that my children promise to be on their best behaviour for at least a month.'

The twins promptly apologised to Mr Brock and promised to behave for one month. But Alfie didn't believe they'd manage even for one *day*!

Then Mrs Tucker invited the rocking-horse mender, and the railway cat, to join the family for a cream tea at the cottage. As they were leaving the workshop Mr Brock turned to look at Rex.

'I must say, Rex is very handsome with his makeshift mane and tail,' he exclaimed.

'Miaow!' cried Alfie. What a fib, Mr Brock!

Anyhow, another alarm over, thought Alfie. What would tomorrow bring?

6

Another Scare

There was an air of excitement about the station as news that Mr Brock had almost completed work on Rex spread. Passengers talked about the horse.

'I must pop into the workshop to see Rex before he leaves,' said one.

'You'll have to give Rex a good send-off, Fred.'

'Mr Brock's going to miss him.'

'Alfie is sure to miss him too.'

'It's funny how that horse has caught people's imagination,' said Hack.

'Not funny at all,' said Fred. 'They all realise he's unique.'

It was half-term holiday and train-spotters were out in force. Clutching note books and pens or pencils they stood in small groups at the far end of the platforms, checking numbers as trains passed.

Once or twice Alfie noticed a man, dressed in a long black coat with a velvet collar, striding about the station. The man wasn't interested in train-spotting, but looked intently at everything on the station, even at the posters on the walls.

Alfie thought he looked a jolly sort of man so he started following him round. The man seemed glad of Alfie's company. Once he stopped and bent down to have a word with the railway cat. 'I think this station will do very nicely,' he said.

'Miaow!' said Alfie. Nicely for what?

After a time Alfie made his way to the booking office. He found Hack talking to Brown.

'I can't understand why that man is spending so much time at our station,' said Hack. 'It looks very suspicious to me.'

Another Scare

'Oh, come off it, Hack!' cried Brown. 'You'll be accusing that little old lady who stepped off the last train of having designs on Rex. I've already said, if the man had been interested in the old rocking-horse, he would have made straight for Mr Brock's instead of spending so much time here.'

Hack shook his head. 'I'm not taking any chances,' he said stubbornly. 'Fred doesn't want to be disturbed this morning, but all the same I'm going to interrupt him and ask his advice.'

'Miaow!' said Alfie quietly. I'm sure you're wrong about the man.

Alfie followed Hack into Fred's office. After he had listened to Hack, Fred said, 'Oh dear! I'm sorry you've been bothered, Hack. I forgot to inform you that we were expecting a special visitor today. He's a famous television producer, who wants to use our station as a location for a new film.'

Alfie miaowed with relief and pleasure at this news.

'Hello, old chap,' said Fred. 'Didn't notice you. I'm sure the railway cat will be needed in the film. You might earn enough money for extra fish and cream. What do you think of that?'

'Miaow!' cried Alfie as he jumped up at Fred's legs. I think I will make an exceptionally good actor!

'You'd better get along, Hack, and see if the producer needs any assistance. Tell him I'll join him when I've finished this urgent job.'

Alfie decided he had left Mr Brock on his own long enough. He turned to go, but halted in the doorway. His nose quivered and his tail twitched.

'What's the matter, Alfie?' asked Fred. He sniffed. 'Something's burning!' he yelled as he got hastily to his feet and made for the door.

As they all rushed out on to the platform they could see a cloud of smoke over the village.

'It's coming from the far end,' shouted Hack.

'Oh no!' cried Fred. 'It can't be. It couldn't *possibly* be . . .!'

Alfie hesitated no longer. He was off like an arrow from a bow. Don't panic, he told himself. The fire might not be at Mr Brock's after all.

His way was blocked by a small group of

people who coughed and spluttered as dense smoke from burning fat rose higher in the air. With eyes smarting, Alfie slipped between a forest of human legs to find smoke and flames pouring out of the fish and chip shop, which was only three doors away from the rocking-horse mender's workshop!

Alfie caught sight of the owner of the shop, and his wife, watching helplessly as the firemen got busy with hoses. He was glad when he heard someone one call out, 'No one's been hurt!' (But Alfie could hardly bear the thought of all that lovely fish going up in smoke!)

The railway cat got a thorough drenching as he shot past the firemen. He found Mr Brock standing in front of his house watching the commotion.

The old man was shaking. 'It's all right now, Alfie,' he called out in a quavering voice. 'I was just about to drag Rex out of the workshop in case the fire spread when a fireman called to tell me there is no danger as the fire is now under control.'

He mopped his forehead with a handkerchief. 'I've shut the door and window to keep out the smoke. It would be terrible if Rex was damaged just when he's nearly ready to leave. Really, I never know what's going to happen next!'

Alfie, purring loudly, weaved in and out of Mr Brock's legs.

'My word, you are wet!' exclaimed the old man. 'Come inside.'

As he rubbed Alfie down with an old towel, Mr Brock said, 'Tuesday's my fish and chip day, so there'll be very little lunch for us today I fear.'

But he was wrong. At that moment a neighbour came down the passage and into the workshop. 'I've got a nice big cottage pie in my oven, Mr Brock,' she said. 'I'll bring some along in half an hour or so, and there'll be a portion for Alfie as well.'

'Prrr ... rrr ... rr ...' went Alfie. He had sampled Mrs Morris's cottage pies on previous occasions.

'That's very neighbourly of you, Mrs Morris,' said Mr Brock.

The fire at the fish and chip shop was almost extinguished by the time Mrs Morris reappeared with the cottage pie.

'Eat it while it's hot,' she said. She stopped on her way out to gaze at Rex. 'I can't take my eyes off that horse when I come in here,' she said. 'He's such a handsome animal.'

'You won't be seeing him much longer, Mrs Morris,' said the rocking-horse mender sadly.

'Well, Mr Brock, you've got plenty of other work to occupy you,' said Mrs Morris briskly. 'Those two over there for instance.' She pointed to two old dappled-grey fairground horses which were in very poor condition.

'Oh yes,' said Mr Brock, brightening up. 'I've got hours and hours of work on those two.'

With many thanks from Mr Brock and purrs from Alfie, Mrs Morris left them to their meal. The cottage pie was excellent. Afterwards Mr Brock lay down on the camp bed and Alfie curled up along-side him. 'Prrr . . . rrr . . . rrr . . .' he sang as Mr Brock tried to doze off.

The old man raised his head to look down at Alfie. 'Really, Alfie!' he laughed. 'You keep me awake in the daytime as well as at night!'

Another Scare

Alfie tried to stay still as he gazed at Rex. During the past few weeks Alfie had watched Mr Brock performing expert 'surgery' on Rex. The day arrived when the last coat of paint had been put on, after which Mr Brock had dabbed large black spots on Rex's body and painted a white diamond on his forehead. When the paint had dried, Rex had been fitted with a new leather saddle and bridle and gleaming brass stirrups.

It was obvious to Alfie that Rex's transformation was almost complete. Soon the old rocking-horse would be seen safely off at the station – and there would be nothing more for Alfie to worry about.

7

Alfie is taken for a Ride

Mr Brock rose early next morning. Alfie stretched out and clenched and unclenched his claws before rolling over and falling off the camp bed.

Mr Brock laughed. 'Come on, sleepy-head,' he said, 'this is an important day. First breakfast, then I'll finish work on Rex.'

'Miaow!' cried Alfie. Feeling very excited he joined the rocking-horse mender for breakfast in the house. Back in the workshop after the meal, Mr Brock walked round the old horse and studied him from every angle. 'There's only one more job to be done,' he announced. 'What's that, Alfie?'

'Miaow!' sang Alfie. He's minus mane and tail, of course.

'A new mane and tail for Rex,' said Mr Brock, smiling.

He picked up some long black horsehair, and made a mane for the horse, shaping it to fit down the neck. Then he cut some more horsehair for a tail. When these had been securely fixed and the rocking-horse mender could find nothing more to be done, he phoned the station and asked Fred to come along to the workshop.

Fred soon arrived, with Hack. 'I wasn't going to miss this,' said Hack.

'My word, Mr Brock, you have done a marvellous job,' said Fred as he stood back to admire the rocking-horse. He turned to Hack. 'Fit for a junk shop, did you say, Hack? Are you now prepared to eat your words?'

Hack grinned. 'All right, I'll have words for my supper tonight,' he said.

'I've enjoyed every minute of working on Rex,' said Mr Brock, 'and the thought of him leaving the country makes me shudder. I wouldn't mind so much if he was going back to his old home.'

'It's a shame he's got to be sold,' said Fred. 'But, whatever happens to him, I hope he will continue to give pleasure to children – and to grown-ups.'

'We'll all miss you, Rex,' said Hack as he gave the horse a friendly pat.

Fred looked at his watch. 'Time to go back to work,' he said. 'Day after tomorrow, Mr Brock, we'll collect Rex for his train journey to the auction rooms. In the meantime, it would be a good idea if you lined the bottom of the crate with more shavings.'

'I'll see to that,' promised Mr Brock as he opened the door for them. 'Staying, Alfie?'

'Miaow!' said Alfie. Please.

After breakfast next morning they returned to the workshop. Mr Brock examined the empty crate still standing in a corner. 'It does need more packing,' he said. He let down the side opening of the crate and started to bundle

in shavings, sawdust and rolled-up papers.
'It wouldn't do to risk Rex being damaged
in transit and spoiling all my hard work,' he said.
Alfie jumped into the crate and vigorously

kneaded the packing with his paws. Then he curled up in the hollow he had made and looked up at Mr Brock.

'Miaow!' he said. It's very comfortable in here.

'Come out of there, Alfie,' laughed Mr Brock. 'We don't want to lose you as well as Rex.' Alfie pushed his nose right down between his paws. 'Now then, you heard me. Out you come,' coaxed Mr Brock.

Alfie was just about to oblige when there was a sharp rap on the door and two men, both in overalls, entered the workshop. Alfie stayed where he was.

'Good morning, Mr Brock,' said one man.

Alfie peeped out of the crate and immediately recognised the men who had asked Hack so many questions, and whom Alfie had observed walking slowly past Mr Brock's. This could be catastrophic, thought the railway cat!

'There's been a change of plan,' the man continued. 'The old rocking-horse is wanted at the auction rooms a day earlier, so instead of going by rail tomorrow we have been ordered to transport him by road today.'

The Railway Cat and the Horse

Mr Brock looked bewildered as the man handed him a document. 'Here you are,' he said. 'Authority to collect one antique rocking-horse, name of Rex.'

The rocking-horse mender glanced at the paper. 'This seems to be in order,' he said slowly, 'but Fred didn't say anything about it yesterday.'

'He didn't know about it then,' was the reply. 'Reason for the change of plan is that there will be a wealthy bidder at tomorrow's auction, and the horse must be there in good time.'

'I'd prefer to get in touch with Fred, if you don't mind,' said Mr Brock, in a flurry.

'No need for that,' said the man sharply. 'Please give us a hand with the crate. We've brought a truck along with us.'

Alfie, almost hidden by the packing, crouched in a corner of the crate as the loading took place. He only just managed to escape being flattened by the rockers. He shook with fright as the crate, with himself and Rex inside, was securely fastened, then wheeled down the passage and lifted into a waiting van.

Alfie is taken for a Ride

One man jumped into the driving seat, the other into the passenger seat and within half a minute they were off. Not for one moment did Alfie believe they were bound for the auction rooms. He had thought these men looked untrustworthy when he had first set eyes on them at the station, and he had been proved right. What would happen to Rex – and to Alfie himself?

Mr Brock had been duped. Somehow the robbers had managed to obtain all the information required for them to steal Rex at the right moment. With his ear towards a crack in the side of the crate, Alfie caught snatches of the men's conversation.

'That was a piece of cake!' laughed the driver.

'You're telling me,' said the other. 'We'll be at the airport in record time. Soon this old rocking-horse will be thousands of miles away, and we'll collect a generous rake-off.'

Alfie felt trapped and helpless. The van was driven at speed but occasionally had to slow down. When he could, to relieve his tension, Alfie reached up and clawed at a very small splinter of wood which he had noticed underneath Rex's belly. After what seemed ages the van suddenly pulled up with a jerk and Alfie fell down flat.

'Keep calm, it's the police!' he heard the driver hiss to his mate.

The rear van door was thrown open and someone – must be a policeman, thought Alfie – climbed in and called out, 'We're checking all vehicles.' Alfie jumped as he heard a sharp rap on the side of the crate. 'What have you got inside here?' said the policeman.

'A refrigerator,' was the driver's prompt reply.

'Well . . .' began the policeman.

He was interrupted by a voice from outside the van, 'You're wanted here for a moment, sergeant.'

With an order, 'Switch off your engine,' the policeman jumped out of the van to join his colleague. At that moment Alfie, in despair, hurled himself against the side of the crate and, scratching frantically, howled and howled.

'A refrigerator *howling*?' Alfie heard the policeman shout as he climbed back into the van. 'Let's see what you've really got in your van.'

The crate was unloaded on to the road. Alfie blinked when it was opened and he and Rex were revealed. He noticed first the two sullen men being held by police.

'Well, well, well,' said the first policeman. 'A rocking-horse and a cat.' He lifted the railway cat out of the crate. 'How did you get in there?' he asked.

'Miaow!' said Alfie. Rex and I were being taken for a ride.

'Does he belong to you?' asked the policeman turning to the robbers.

'No!' snarled one, with a baleful glance at Alfie.

'Fancy being caught because of a stupid cat,' said the other man.

'A very clever cat, you should say,' said the policeman. He stared at Alfie. 'I'm sure I've seen you before somewhere.'

Alfie purred. I've often been in the news, he wanted to tell him.

'We'll soon find out more about you, and the rocking-horse,' said the policeman.

Soon they were all at the police station. As Alfie lapped some milk he heard voices all around him, phones ringing and people coming and going. He enjoyed his time in police custody. He was given plenty to eat and drink and was congratulated time after time for alerting the police.

Alfie wasn't in the least worried about getting back home. He'd been lost before, and Fred had always managed to find him. Sure enough, after several long telephone calls, the officer in charge came across to Alfie, who was sitting on a counter contentedly watching everything going on.

'We've traced your owners,' said the officer. 'You're Alfie, the railway cat.'

'Miaow!' said Alfie. Of course I am.

'I should have recognised you immediately, as I've seen your picture in the papers and on television. We could certainly do with a clever cat like you at *our* station,' he said.

'Miaow!' said Alfie hastily. Thank you, but Fred couldn't manage without me at my station.

Later that evening when Fred arrived, Alfie made a joyous rush at his friend. Fred scooped him up and squeezed him gently.

'Fine cat, that,' said the officer. 'Helped to catch two criminals who've been on the run for months. He can go home with you, but we'll have to keep the rocking-horse a little longer.'

'Well done, Alfie,' said Fred. The railway cat purred contentedly as he sat upright in the front passenger seat of his friend's car and was driven back to the station.

In the staff room Alfie jumped up on to the comfortable chair, curled himself into a ball, put his chin on his tail and closed his eyes. Catching criminals was an exhausting job, he thought.

He opened one eye as he heard Fred lock the door behind him, but Alfie had no objection to being shut up in his own staff room. He was soon fast asleep.

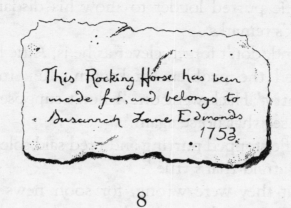

This Rocking Horse has been
made for, and belongs to
Susannah Lane Edmonds
1753.

8

An Important Discovery

Next day everyone wanted to hear about the
attempted robbery and Alfie's part in the rescue.
'If it hadn't been for Alfie, goodness knows
where Rex would be by now,' said one
passenger.

Others joined in, 'Alfie is always ready for any
emergency.'

'He's almost human!'

Fred beamed at the railway cat, but Hack said,
'Oh, it's Alfie this and Alfie that. There's no
end to hearing about that cat!'

Alfie purred louder to show his disdain for Hack's remarks.

'And, don't forget, clever as he is, Alfie hasn't solved the problem of keeping Rex in this country,' Hack went on. 'I don't suppose we'll ever see that horse again.'

Alfie stopped purring and Fred said solemnly, 'I'm afraid that's true.'

But they were wrong, for soon news came that Rex was being sent back to the workshop by rail, so that Mr Brock could examine him for possible damage. Alfie made sure of being at the workshop when Rex arrived.

The rocking-horse mender started straight away on a thorough examination of Rex. To Alfie this seemed to take a long time. At last Mr Brock made a final check for any flaws by running his hand over the horse's smooth body surface.

'Well, Alfie,' he said. 'I think I can pass Rex as in perfect condition.' Then, 'Ouch! What's this?' he cried as he held up a blood-stained finger tip.

The old man bent down to look underneath

the horse. 'Why! It's a splinter! However did I miss that? And *scratch* marks!'

Mr Brock looked hard at Alfie, who stared back at him. 'Oh, well, don't worry, Alfie,' he said. 'No real harm has been done. I'll soon repair it.'

A relieved Alfie jumped on to the platform underneath Rex, but the old man laughed as he gently pushed him aside. 'How do you expect me to do the repairs if you get in my way?' he said.

So Alfie sat on the floor. Mr Brock started by lightly sandpapering the scratched area. Suddenly he stopped, adjusted his spectacles and peered closer. 'And what's this?' he exclaimed. 'Would you believe it, there's a small crack as well. I really must have my eyesight tested.'

By this time Mr Brock was lying on his back underneath Rex. Alfie craned his neck, puzzled, as Mr Brock picked up a penknife and carefully inserted it into the crack. 'There's something wedged in the crack, Alfie,' he cried excitedly.

Alfie moved closer as Mr Brock probed

further and eventually pulled out of the crack a folded-up piece of yellowed paper. His face was flushed as he went over to the bench and gently smoothed out the creases in the paper. Then, with trembling hands, he held it up to the light.

'It's handwritten, Alfie,' cried the old man. 'Just listen to this.' He began to read as he peered at the faded lettering:

'This rocking horse has been made for, and belongs to, Susannah Jane Edmonds. 23 April 1753.'

He waved the paper at Alfie. 'Wonderful news, Alfie,' he cried. 'Wonderful.'

But Alfie couldn't understand why his friend should be so elated over a mere scrap of paper. Now if there had been a £50 note, or even a £5 note, inside Rex, that would have helped the family fortunes just a little, wouldn't it? It would have been better than nothing.

'How lucky that you scratched at Rex as you did, Alfie,' went on Mr Brock. 'This scrap of paper might never have been found but for you. You realise what an important document it is?'

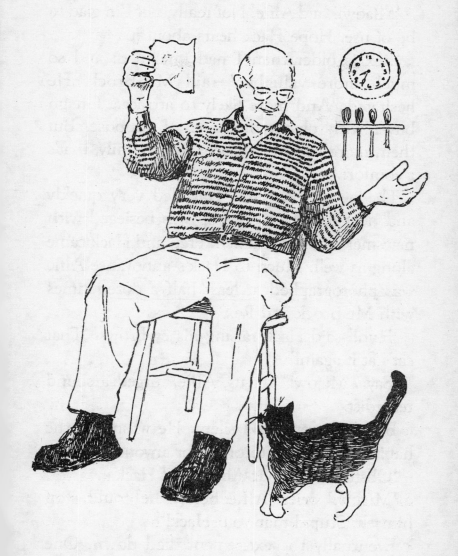

'Miaow!' said Alfie. Not really, but I'm glad to be of use. Hope Hack hears about it.

'Rex is older than I had imagined, and so much more valuable,' said Mr Brock. He hesitated. 'And more likely to attract a foreign buyer with plenty of money, I suppose. But then, more money will help Rex's family, that's a comfort.'

The news about Rex travelled very quickly and next day the workshop was besieged with newsmen and cameramen. Fred and Hack came along as well. Much to Hack's annoyance Alfie was photographed at least half a dozen times with Mr Brock and Rex.

'Huh!' said Hack raising his eyebrows. 'That cat's at it again!'

'Say, "Miaow!" for us, Alfie,' urged a sound recordist.

But Alfie remained silent. He wasn't in the habit of miaowing to order for anyone.

'Obstinate cat, our Alfie,' said Hack.

'Miaow!' cried Alfie before he could stop himself. Stupid man, our Hack!

Eventually the excitement died down. One

week passed and then another and nothing was heard about Rex's delivery to the auction rooms.

Mr Brock was hopeful and despondent by turns. He would mutter to himself and to Alfie. One day it would be, 'Perhaps the family will be able to keep Rex after all.' Another day he would say, 'They must be waiting for a very wealthy buyer to come forward.' Now and then, just for fun, Alfie jumped up on to Rex's back and, purring loudly, allowed Mr Brock to rock him to and fro.

One day when Alfie was in the workshop, they were surprised by a visit from the Government official who had admired Rex. The man was very interested in the scrap of paper and wanted to hear first-hand about the discovery. Although he didn't understand everything that was being discussed, Alfie listened intently as Mr Brock and the official held a long conversation.

After a time the man said, 'Well, Mr Brock, I will see what can be done about Rex. In my opinion that horse is a national heirloom and should remain in this country.'

He nodded to Alfie as he left the workshop. 'And that cat should be given a medal, or at least salmon suppers for a whole year!' he said smiling.

'Miaow!' cried Alfie as he followed the man to the door. You're a man after my own heart. I'll have the salmon, please.

Time passed and there was still no news about the fate of the rocking-horse, but one day Mr Brock came running to the station.

'Good news! Good news!' he shouted, as he tried to make himself heard above the noise of an outgoing train. When the train had left and silence reigned he went on, 'Everything's going to be all right. Rex is returning to his own home!'

'How's that?' asked Fred, as the staff and Alfie gathered round to listen.

'Our friend, the Government official, has used his influence to persuade an Historic Preservation Society to take the matter in hand,' Mr Brock said.

'Good for him,' said Fred.

Mr Brock smiled and nodded. 'I understand

Rex's owners are to be given an allowance so that they can continue living in the old mansion,' he said. 'One condition is that the house and gardens must be opened to the public on payment of an entrance fee.'

'That will help the family finances,' said Hack.

'Yes,' said Mr Brock. 'There will be many antique items for the public to view.'

'And Rex will be the principal attraction!' shouted Fred.

Everyone cheered and laughed as Mr Brock said, 'I'm sure he will. I'll have to get the crate ready again, but this time Rex will be going *home.*'

'By rail, I hope?' said Fred smiling.

'Of course!' said the rocking-horse mender. 'I wouldn't let him out of my workshop otherwise.'

'Miaow!' sang Alfie as he rolled over and over at Mr Brock's feet.

'Pity they can't take that cat as well. Put him on show,' said Hack.

'I'll make quite sure Alfie isn't shut inside the crate again,' said Mr Brock. 'In his own way he's just as valuable as Rex.'

When the time came for Rex's departure the station was thronged with people wanting to give him a good send-off. Alfie hung back as the guard blew his whistle and the train with Rex on board started to move slowly out of the station.

Now that Rex had gone everything seemed dull and uninteresting to Alfie. What should he do? He moped about the station until Fred said, 'Cheer up, for goodness sake, Alfie. You're making us all feel miserable.'

'And get on with a bit of mice catching. That's what you're here for,' cried Hack.

'Don't be hard on Alfie,' said Fred. 'Like all of us he's missing Rex. Pity we won't see that horse again.'

'And why not?' said Hack. 'We can pay to go and see him when he's put on show, same as anyone else, can't we?'

'That's the first sensible suggestion I've heard from you for a long time,' said Fred. 'A visit won't be possible just yet as I understand the house needs considerable improvement first. But I will organise an outing to go and see Rex on the very first day the house is open to the public.'

An outing to see Rex in his own home? thought Alfie, excited. That would be something to look forward to. Then a disturbing thought struck him. Would Fred be sure to include the railway cat on the outing?

'Miaow . . . Miaow . . .' he said anxiously as he looked up at Fred.

'What's the matter, Alfie?' said Fred. 'I promise we'll take you along, if that's what you're worrying about.'

The Railway Cat and the Horse

Alfie was content. He knew that Fred would keep his promise.
And he did.